I0735918

REWRITING THE RULES

BOOK SEVEN OF *REVIN'S HEART*

STEVEN D. BREWER

Copyright © 2023 by Steven D. Brewer

All rights reserved.

No part of this book may be reproduced or transmitted in any form or by any means, electronic or mechanical, except for the purpose of review and/or reference, without explicit permission in writing from the publisher.

Cover design copyright © 2023 by Niki Lenhart
nikilen-designs.com

Published by Water Dragon Publishing
waterdragonpublishing.com

ISBN 978-1-959804-97-0 (Trade Paperback)

FIRST EDITION

10 9 8 7 6 5 4 3 2 1

AUTHOR'S NOTE

Revin's Heart is my debut work as a new author. When I first wrote "The Third Time's the Charm", I had a sense for the larger world in which it was set, but I had not fully plotted out where the story would go. Having the opportunity to tell the rest of the story has been immensely gratifying. But I could not have done it without support of many people.

I'm grateful to my editor Steven Radecki who gave me enough to rope to ... No, who trusted me enough to commit to publishing the rest of the series having seen only the first two parts. I have learned a vast amount — and have had a huge amount of fun — writing the rest of the series with the support and partnership of him and Water Dragon Publishing.

I need to also acknowledge the enthusiastic cheerleading of my review team, in particular Francesca Forrest and Martha Allard, who've read the episodes as they've come out and provided unflagging support and encouragement.

I would be remiss to not also mention my brother Philip and my son Daniel who are my trusted beta readers. They read my earliest manuscripts, while they're still sketchy, to help me identify problems with story structure and pacing. And to offer both helpful comments and unfailing mockery.

And there's my mom, Lucy, who reads everything I write if only to tell me how everything I do is perfect. Though even she admits that some things are more perfect than others.

And my wife Alisa. She won't read anything I write, but is always supportive and helps manage my life so that I have the time and attention to devote to my new career as an author.

Finally, thank you to you — all my devoted readers and fans — for coming with me on this adventure!

REWRITING THE RULES

R EVIN ARRIVED PROMPTLY at 6 bells at the antechamber of the king in response to a summons. He went to surrender his sword, like usual, but they just waved him straight through. He had typically waited for hours before being admitted to the King's presence but he was ushered instantly into a dressing room where the King stood, being fitted for a fresh military uniform.

He motioned Revin to enter. Revin stood at attention.

"Do you wish a report on the peace talks, Your Majesty?" Revin asked.

"I regret, Sir Revin," the King began. "That I need to communicate something of importance to you."

Revin leaned forward, all attention.

"While you have been pursuing peace, the Kingdom has been preparing for war," the King said. "This morning, our full armies have launched an assault on Havelock."

"What?" Revin said, dumbfounded.

"It was obvious they had intended to attack Harway from the beginning. I couldn't let that pass."

"So ..." Revin said, grasping for thoughts. "So my entire effort has been a diversion? You used me to pretend to offer peace only while you gathered your forces for an attack?"

"Once we took the eternite mine," the King said. "It was a foregone conclusion we would be at war. I received word this morning that the mine has been taken and is ours. Upon that notice, I ordered our armed forces to attack in full."

Revin just stood there, mute. Then he felt his face flush as his anger began to rise.

"I'm sorry if you feel deceived, Sir Revin," the King said. "But once Havelock attacked us, there was really no path forward but war."

"Then what are your orders, Your Majesty?" Revin said, stiffly.

"Your loyalty does you credit, Sir Revin," the King replied. "The peace talks are now ended and We will make no further call upon your services. The forces are away and there is no longer any call for secrecy. You may do as you choose. You may notify your staff. And you may tell the delegates, if you so desire. Though they will undoubtedly know soon enough."

And with a wave the King dismissed Revin.

"By your grace, Your Majesty," Revin said with a bow and, turning, departed.

Revin headed straight to the offices of the Special Envoy.

Hannah was already there, hard at work preparing the agenda for the day's meetings. "Good morning, Revin," she sang out when he came in.

"You won't think so after you hear this," he said.

"What?" she said, stopping and looking up.

"The peace talks are over. The King has been using us as a diversion," Revin said. "Harway has dispatched its armies to attack Havelock."

Hannah threw her quill across the room where it splattered against the wall.

"Oh, Revin," she said. "I'm so sorry. You must be livid."

"I think I'm still in shock," Revin said. "I guess we should inform the delegations today."

"We were making progress!" Hannah grumbled angrily.

"I thought so too," Revin said. "Let's get this over with."

Two hours later, the delegates filed into the hall and Revin could immediately tell that everyone had already heard the news. He noticed one empty chair and percceived that Momo was not attending. He cleared his throat and addressed the delegates.

"As you have all seemingly heard, I have been directed by King Reginald to conclude the peace talks," Revin said. "This was not my choice, but I serve at the pleasure of the King and I fulfill my duties to the best of my abilities. Our meetings are hereby adjourned. I thank you for your contributions. May you all travel safely in these uncertain times."

"You are an utter disgrace," Count Cindakor said, rising. "You brought us here under false pretenses and wasted weeks of our time. For nothing! Although we may agree on nothing, I feel confident that the delegates from Havelock will agree with me that you deserve censure and repudiation for your abjectly dishonest performance."

Everyone stood and silently filed out of the salon.

Revin sighed and turned to Hannah. "Thank you for everything," Revin said. "If we accomplished anything, it was thanks to you. You put together a great team and did yeoman's work to keep us moving forward. Thank you."

"It was all you, Revin," Hannah said, in her gravelly rasp. "We never would have even gotten them to the table if you hadn't pulled out all the stops. I'm glad I got to work with you, even if we don't get to go all the way. Thank you."

They nodded to each other, then departed, going separate directions.

Revin was walking through the courtyard heading back to his room when someone shoved a bag over his head. He felt his arms gripped on both sides. Stumbling, he was dragged through the door into the park. He struggled and tried to yell when someone punched him in the gut. He would have doubled over, but for the grip on his arms holding him up.

The bag was pulled off his head and he was thrown onto the ground in a wooded area of the park. Count Cindakor and a handful of his associates stood over him.

"You freak," the Count sneered at him. "You monstrosity. You're going to get what's coming to you now."

Count Cindakor's men began kicking him. Revin tried to cover his head when someone stomped on his face. He tried turning over, but they kept kicking his arms and legs and ribs. He tried to focus as panic threatened to overwhelm him. He closed his eyes and tried to find an etheric stream as the blows rained on him. He managed to make an attachment to a low tree branch which pulled away and then snapped back when he released it. The men turned when the branch suddenly swung toward them.

Revin scrabbled to his feet while they were distracted and began to run. The men gave chase. Revin had never run so hard before, his sight darkening to tunnel vision as he tried desperately to get away.

After a few moments, he heard them laughing as he ran away. He found a dense thicket and curled up inside, shivering and crying with pain and fear. He found he'd wet himself in his terror. He lay there miserably for a half hour or more until he was sure they must have left.

He crept slowly back to the courtyard, watching for anyone waiting for him, then he slipped up the stairs to his room to be safe. But when he got to the top of the stairs, he found his trunk sitting out in the hallway, open, with his belongings thrown inside. He tried his key in the door, but the lock had been changed. Revin sat down on the floor and broke down into sobs.

Eventually, Revin stood and tucked everything into the trunk. He dragged it down the steps and went out the side entrance to the guards.

"Can I get a coach to the aerodrome?" he asked.

"I'm sorry, Sir Revin," the guard replied. "We've been informed your access to the coach service has been revoked."

"I can pay," Revin said.

"We don't request private coaches," the guard said. Revin must have looked devastated because the guard took pity on him. "Normally. Let me see what I can do."

Twenty minutes later, a private coach arrived. The coachman put Revin's trunk in the storage compartment and held the door for Revin to climb into the coach. Revin settled into the back, profoundly grateful for small favors.

When he arrived at the aerodrome, he was unsurprised to find that *Pamela's Panties* was no longer available for his use and had been turned over to the nobleman who had originally ordered her. He inquired about the next seat available to fly to Candlemain and was told that he could get a small compartment on a flight leaving the next day. He paid and then sat on a bench and began the long wait.

After a bit, Revin went to the bathroom and looked at himself in the mirror. He had huge bruises on his face and a black eye. His arms and ribs were also bruised. By a miracle, he didn't seem to have any broken bones. His hair was full of dirt and twigs. He cleaned himself as best as he could and changed into clean clothes.

He got out Momo's journal and, after paging through what she'd written previously, he got out his pen and began to write.

He poured out his soul: his anger, his uncertainties, and his fears. As he wrote, he realized he'd never been so angry before. He felt like he understood better why Will didn't trust the nobility. Revin still felt conflicted, but he was finally becoming willing to admit to himself how strong his feelings were for Momo and how important she was to him.

"Did you hear?" someone said, coming into the waiting room. "Prince Stewart is finally married!"

"Really?" the man behind the counter said. "Everyone's been wondering who will finally catch him. Who is it?"

"Someone I've never heard of," the other man replied. "Someone from Belleriand. Momray? Momoray? Something like that."

"Lady Momoire?" asked Revin, stunned.

"Yeah! That's it," the man said. "Their marriage will cement the alliance between Harway and Belleriand against Havelock."

Revin looked at the journal he'd been writing and wanted to scratch or tear out everything he'd just written. His throat closed up and he felt his gorge rise. He closed the journal, put away his pen, and sat on the bench staring at the ground. His mind stopped working for a while.

"Excuse me, sir," someone said, shaking his shoulder.

Revin had fallen asleep.

"Excuse me. The waiting room is closing for the night."

"Can't I wait here?" Revin asked.

"I'm sorry sir," the man said. "We'll open tomorrow morning at 6 bells."

Revin dragged his trunk out as they locked the door behind him, then he dragged it off the aerodrome and huddled in a wooded area. It already felt chilly. Revin shivered in the dark. Revin wrapped another coat from his trunk around him. The wind began to rise and rain started falling. Revin pressed his back up against the trunk and pulled the coat over his head as he broke down and wept. It was a long and sleepless night as the rain, trickling, found its way in and soaked him to the bone.

•　　　•　　　•

The next morning dawned cloudy and misty. Revin dragged his trunk back to the passenger terminal. They had coffee, for which Revin was endlessly grateful. At 7 bells, they announced boarding for the *Bellewhether* to Candlemain via Belleriand. Revin started when he heard that he would be traveling through Belleriand and considered trying to find some other way to go. With no other options available, he dragged his trunk on board and found his cabin — the poorest cabin at the very end of the airship.

Once in his cabin, even as the airship was still rising, he stripped off his wet clothes and put something dry from his trunk. Then he collapsed and slept for many hours.

•　　　•　　　•

He awoke when the *Bellewhether* landed in Belleriand. Revin looked out as soldiers surrounded the airship. As passengers disembarked, they were searched and their names checked against a list. A team of soldiers came up the ramp. Revin couldn't hear what they said, but from their expressions he could see that they were demanding to search the airship and were being barred from doing so by the crew. Revin shrank back into his seat and shivered, remembering the last time he endured the tender mercies of the Belleriand intelligence service. He rubbed his wrists reflexively, ducking down when he spotted soldiers walking around the airship looking in at the windows. They were probably too low to see anything, but Revin wasn't taking any chances.

After what seemed like an eternity, but which in truth was only about a half hour, the soldiers stepped back off the ramp, and the *Bellewhether* lifted off and headed west, over the ocean, bound for Candlemain.

Revin looked out the window remembering his first trip by airship in the *Madeline*. He remembered being fascinated by the view out the window, the blue towlines of the remmers drawing them forward over the boundless ocean. He felt a moment of peace and almost smiled, But then the reality of running away with his tail between his legs brought him back to earth and he sighed deeply.

The sun had just set when the *Bellewhether* touched down on Candlemain. There was no aerodrome — just an open field at the outskirts of town. Revin dragged his trunk down the ramp and looked at the seemingly peaceful seaside village. He knew first hand that the intelligence services of both Havelock and Belleriand were present. But he didn't see any alternative but to wait until the pirates came to resupply.

Dragging his trunk, he made his way to Mama Kane's boarding house. He'd heard pirates talk about her as being honest and offering good hospitality. A big draw was that her house was close to the harbor and offered a good view of the pier. Revin dragged his trunk up and found her chatting with guests on the patio.

Mama Kane kept her white hair under a colorful bandana. An older, large and heavy-set woman with rough, pink skin, her tiny, beady eyes sat almost lost in folds of flesh, but a big, wide smile with one gold tooth shone right in front.

"Dear me, young man," she said, catching sight of Revin coming into the light. "Did you get in a fight with someone?"

"Yeah," Revin admitted. "All six of them."

"Well, if anyone tries to give you any trouble here, you let me know about it, you hear?"

"Yes, ma'am," Revin said.

"Call me Mama," she said. "Everyone does."

"Yes, Mama."

"Now, let's find you a room. Haven't I seen you here before?"

"I've never stayed, but I might have come with Grip before."

"Ah! I thought you looked familiar. I've got just the room for you. You'll be wanting to keep an eye on the pier, I'll wager. This room at the end is good. You can pull a chair out and sit right here to watch."

Revin accepted the key and listened while she pointed out the amenities of the room.

"Now if you need anything just holler, you hear?"

"Yes, Mama."

•　　　•　　　•

Revin awoke on Thursday morning and got up, still stiff and sore from his bruises, even after three days. He dragged a chair out in front of his room where he could put his feet up and watch the shore and the pier, to await the arrival of the *Little WormMaid* — the pirate's small sailboat that they used to provision themselves, although Revin wasn't certain they would come this week. He was sitting in the chilly dawn air, before the land breeze set up when Mama brought him a cup of coffee. He nodded his thanks, not wanting to disturb the morning's peace. Then he saw her.

She wore all black: an elegant black hat with a veil and a long, formal black dress that stood out among the colorful island attire. And, even at a long distance, Revin knew instantly who it was. She walked directly up to him and planted herself in front of him.

"What are you doing here?" Momo said.

"Milady," Revin said.

"Are we back to that?"

"You're the one who got married," Revin said.

"That wasn't my decision," Momo said. "I didn't have any choice! It doesn't change how I feel. Or how Stewart feels about you!"

"I'm done with the nobility," Revin said, bitterly. "I got picked up, used, and discarded."

"I'm sorry, Revin," Momo said. "I'm really sorry. But we need you."

"What do you need me for?" Revin said, brandishing his bruised arms, spectacularly purple and yellow, and pointing to his black eye. "A punching bag?"

"Are you going to let them get away with that?" Momo snapped.

"I just don't care anymore," Revin said, standing and turning to go back to his room.

"No!" Momo said, stamping her foot, tears springing from her eyes. "You can't! You're *my* hero. And ... And! And I *order* you to serve me!"

Revin stopped, hearing Momo sniffle, trying not to sob. He paused and closed his eyes. He remembered the Baron warning him to temper his expectations. But, for a long moment, his principles did battle with his heart. For what seemed an eternity, he stood there caught on the horns of the conflict between everything he believed and everything he felt. In a flash, he remembered Momo sliding down the banister. Momo laughing. Momo stroking his hair after his nightmare. Momo taking his hand at the opera. Momo kissing him. And he decided. He turned and dropped to a knee at Momo's feet. He took her hand and pressed his lips to it.

"I once told you I would do anything for you, Milady," Revin said, looking up at her. "And I'm a man of my word. What would you have me do?"

"I need you to be my chief of staff," Momo said. "I'm surrounded by people trying to tell me what to do. I need a right-hand man. I need someone I can trust. And you're the only one I trust."

"I'm yours, Milady," Revin said. "Now and forever."

Revin looked up at Momo, then looked past her and felt a chill go through him. He struggled to his feet.

"Momo," he said, quietly. "We're being watched!"

"Oh," she said. "That's my security detail. I told them to be discreet."

Revin looked farther and saw the *Little WormMaid* approaching the pier in the harbor.

"We had better go meet the *WormMaid* before your bodyguards tangle with the pirates," Revin said.

He took Momo's hand to assist her down the steps. They walked together toward the pier while the pirates tied up the *WormMaid* and began walking down the pier toward the town.

Grip's face was filled with concern when he saw Revin's bruises, but he truly blanched when he saw Momo dressed all in black.

"Who died?" he asked, in a panic. "It's not ..."

"No," Momo said. "It's the King."

"What?!?" Revin said, floored.

"But if the King is dead then who is ..." Grip said.

"It's Stewart."

"But Stewart wasn't first born ..." Grip said.

"His older brother was killed leading the invasion force."

"But if Stewart is King then ... Your Majesty!" Revin said.

Grip looked back and forth between Revin and Momo as the enormity of what Revin had just said began to sink in.

Revin's head spun while he tried to take in what was happening. He began to realize that being Momo's — No! The Queen's! — chief of staff was going to be invested with far more responsibility than he had initially imagined.

"Harway walked into a trap," Queen Momoire said. "Havelock had an Etheric Storm Generator concealed offshore that severely damaged the invasion force and their delegation left another in the palace that was triggered after they left. It flattened the palace, killed the king, and destroyed much of the city."

"What's going to happen?" Revin asked.

"It's anybody's guess at this point — there's total chaos. There will be a summit at Ravensbelth in three days' time," the Queen said. "I came here to find you and bring you to the meeting. I wasn't joking when I said we need you."

"Let me go to Will and the Professor to see if I can get them to come as well," Revin said.

"Three days," Momo said, her lip quivering. "Don't be late."

"No, Your Majesty," Revin said. "I will not fail you."

Revin wanted to hug Momo, who was obviously on the verge of tears, but he held himself back and she pulled herself back together. She headed back to the field and, a few minutes later, they saw her airship rise and head east.

Ham and the others went to provision the pirates while Grip went with Revin to collect his trunk and check out of Mama Kane's.

"You know Will isn't going to want to get involved," Grip said.

"I know what he'll say," Revin said. "But I think I know how to persuade him."

"And what happened to you?" Grip asked. "Did you get in a fight?"

"Yeah, but you should see the other six guys," Revin retorted. "Their boots are all scuffed and covered with my bodily fluids."

"Seriously?"

"Count Cindakor and his flunkies," Revin said. "Once the King was done with me, the gloves came off."

"That bastard," Grip snarled. "He has a lot to answer for."

"Well, but if it hadn't happened, I probably would have still been there and would have died. So there's that."

Grip grabbed Revin and pulled him into a hug.

"I'm sorry for what you went through," Grip said. "But I'm very glad you're with us still."

Revin hugged Grip back and they stayed like that for a long moment. Finally, they separated and Revin went to settle up with Mama Kane while Grip hoisted Revin's trunk on his shoulder like it was nothing and carried it down to the *WormMaid*.

"Thanks, Mama," Revin said, slipping her an extra reggie after paying the bill.

"Oh, you sweet boy!" she said, crushing him in a hug. "You come back again, you hear?"

While Ham and the others finished provisioning and Grip collected the mail, Revin walked through the market. Keeping his eyes open, he went to the stall where the woman sold bound journals. The one he'd liked before with a raven or crow on the cover was still there. Or possibly one just like it. Revin selected it, paid the shy woman, then headed to the pier and boarded the *WormMaid* as Ham and the rest loaded the provisions.

Two hours later, Revin stood in the bow watching the flying fish as the WormMaid approached Kapper Island. He heard a cry go up from an observer on shore and the pirates came charging down to help unload the provisions — or so he thought. They suddenly grabbed him and carried him on their shoulders up to the pirates' base cheering all the while.

"Welcome back, lad!" Will said, coming out and embracing him. "You've been as successful as usual at keeping out of trouble, I see."

"What can I say?" Revin said, blushing with all the attention. "And just wait 'til you hear what I'm doing for my next trick!"

"Oh, no!" Will cried and the crowd roared with laughter and approval. "You can tell me all about it — after the party."

Revin turned around and around, watching the whirl of activity and seeing all the friendly and familiar faces. For the first time in weeks, he felt truly at home. He made the rounds, checking in with everyone and politely declining rum when offered. Eventually, he took a couple of skewers of meat and joined Will and Grip who sat together off to the side.

"Grip won't tell me anything," Will said.

Revin just raised one eyebrow.

"Hmph. Be that way," Will said, feigning grumpiness.

Revin grinned and took another bite of meat as the party became ever more festive with music and dancing fueled by the rum.

"Alright, you pup," Will said finally. "Let's get everyone together and hear your report."

Once everyone was gathered, Revin stood and paced back and forth in front of the room.

"Four days ago, the King summoned me to tell me that he'd been using me as a diversion while he gathered his forces to attack Havelock. And, once he was done with me, he discarded me."

"This is not a surprise to me," Will said. "I'm sorry it happened to you. But I could have told you this would happen. Indeed I think I did tell you."

"You did. But, look. We became pirates because the world has been divided into two classes: the nobles and the commoners. And we fit into neither camp. We're neither noble nor commoner.

"You could argue that there's a third class: those who serve the nobility. But ..."

Revin looked at Will and both shook their heads.

"But you'll learn that if you serve the nobility, you're still a commoner. And, sooner or later, that will be brought home to you.

"OK, boy," Will said. "So what's happened? Don't keep us in the dark."

"The King is dead," Revin said, flatly.

"And who is the new King?"

"Stewart," Revin said. "You know him as ..."

"Words," Will said. "I know."

"But did you know Words got married?" Revin asked. Will looked puzzled.

"Prince Stewart married Lady Momoire," Revin continued. "We now have a true Queen of Belleriand. I have agreed to serve her as her chief of staff."

"So, the King threw you out to be kicked and beaten like a dog," Will said. "And you're already so eager to crawl back to the nobility and lick their feet?"

"Not a bit of it," Revin said with a wink. "What I see is a chance to rewrite the rules. Remember it's not the nobility you hate. They're just playing their part, same as you. It's the rules that divide us. That's what we need to change."

"And how do you propose to do that?" the Professor said.

"Got 'em!" Revin thought with a chuckle. Then, out loud, he said, "Well, let me tell you ..."

He pulled out the journal where he'd begun sketching out his plan and explained his idea.

•   •   •

Two days later, the *Queen of Belleriand* arrived at the Belleriand aerodrome. A detachment of Belthingstone guards saluted Revin smartly as he disembarked. A coach was waiting to take Revin, Will, Grip, and the Professor to Ravensbelth. Two guards took up positions on the coach while the others rode on horseback around the coach as they attracted stares through the streets of the capital.

Youngman, the aged head butler, met them at the grand entrance of Ravensbelth, welcomed them, and led them to a lively reception in the Porcelain Room. Inside were more than a hundred people from the highest echelons of both the Belleriand and Harway nobility.

"Sir Revin Minerson of Devishire," Youngman announced upon his arrival.

Conversation halted. Dead silence fell. Revin swallowed and stepped into the room with as much confidence as he could muster. He recognized few familiar faces. At the far end of the room, he saw King Stewart and Queen Momoire standing together, still wearing the black of mourning.

"Excuse me, Sir Revin," someone said in the silence.

Revin turned, but stepped back when he found himself face-to-face with Count Cindakor.

Count Cindakor bowed deeply. "I would like to publicly apologize for my shameless and unwarranted slanders of your character. They were totally uncalled for, as was my unconscionable attack on your person by my staff. I hope you will accept my sincere apology and my personal word that I will work together with you going forward."

Revin was taken aback, stunned, but recovered quickly.

"Your apology is accepted," Revin said. "Pray think of it no further."

After a moment, Revin reached out his hand and they shook hands to a round of polite applause. Count Cindakor melted back into the crowd. Revin began trying to work his way toward Momo. He bowed to Lady Cecelia along the way. Grip introduced him to his older brother, Cordwin, who looked even more like their father than Grip did. He stood slightly shorter than Grip, but was broader and even more muscular.

Eventually, he reached the end of the room where the King and Queen waited.

"We thank you for coming," Queen Momoire said. "We hope you found the Count's apology to your satisfaction."

"Yes, Your Majesty," Revin said. "I am entirely satisfied, if you are."

Momo's eyes narrowed.

"I would have had him slow roasted over a fire and basted with lemon juice," she said. "But we need his faction too much."

"Sir Revin," the King said. "On behalf of the Kingdom of Harway, We would also offer Our apology. And We are overjoyed you will yet serve Us. We are well pleased."

"Your Majesty," Revin said, bowing deeply.

Revin spent another hour circulating through the crowd, meeting as many people as he could. Finally, as he was starting to fall asleep on his feet, he found Terrier standing at his shoulder.

"Pardon me, Sir Revin," Terrier said with a bow. "Her Majesty has tasked me with leading you to your quarters."

Terrier led Revin to a different room than he had stayed in before. It was much smaller than the luxurious guest room, but felt more comfortable.

"This door communicates directly with her Majesty's quarters," Terrier said, indicating an interior door. "She asked for you to be placed here so as to have you at hand as needed. But she asked me to tell you that she will not call on you this night so that you may rest and prepare yourself for the summit tomorrow. Breakfast will be at 6 bells as usual. Good night, sir."

"Good night," Revin said. "And thank you Terrier."

"It's very good to have you back, sir," Terrier said. "And you know that if you need anything at all, it would be my pleasure to serve you."

Revin looked in the closet and found that, not only was his trunk there, but the clothes had been carefully brushed and hung up. And there was sleeping apparel which, this time, he gratefully put on and then laid down in the comfortable bed. He closed his eyes. But, after a time, he found he just couldn't sleep.

He eventually got up and, wearing pajamas and a robe, made his way through the dark and empty corridors to the botanical garden and sat, alone, near the fountain listening to the music of the water. He looked up at the cloudy night sky and watched bats flit overhead. He sighed. Someone put a hand on his shoulder. He looked up into the face of the Baron.

"Milord!" he said, struggling to stand.

The Baron gently held him in place and smiled, then came around and joined him on the bench.

"Well met, Sir Revin," he said.

"Well met, Milord!"

"I'm glad for us to have a moment to chat before the summit," the Baron said. "And so that I can thank you for standing by my little Momoire."

"You must be very proud," Revin said.

"I'm very proud of all of my children," he said. "And I'm proud of you too."

"Huh?"

The Baron paused for a moment, as though having an internal debate, and then, having resolved it, he leaned back.

"You know that Dirge became our agent. Before we hired him, we vetted him thoroughly, of course. And that means, we also vetted you thoroughly beforehand."

"So ... You knew who I was before Grip introduced me to you?"

"That's right."

"And so you know that I'm ..."

"I've always known."

"Did Dirge know?"

"Yes, he knew. I suspected at the time, he was planning to get you to Havelock where you'd have no options or support and then try to pressure you for sexual favors. He really was not a nice man."

Revin felt like the floor had fallen out from under him.

"I keenly felt for you at the time," the Baron continued. "But I didn't feel like there was anything I could do. And, in spite of everything, you ended up rescuing Griphon. I truly owe you a great debt."

For once in his life, Revin was speechless.

"Do your parents know what's happened to you? Have you been home to see your family since you left?" the Baron asked.

"No," Revin said. "They could never accept that ... that I would never be the docile little girl they wanted. That I wasn't going to let myself be married off to an older man and beaten into submission to bear his children and do his housework."

"That's so sad," the Baron said. "You'd make a good father. Maybe you will someday."

"I ... I wish you were my father," Revin said, in a tiny voice, then started crying as feelings he never knew he had welled up from somewhere deep inside of him.

The Baron tousled Revin's hair and then pulled him into a hug as Revin tried to master his emotions.

Finally, Revin pulled away, wiping his eyes, and stood. "I think I'd better try to get some sleep, Milord," Revin said.

"Good night, young man."

Revin walked back to his room and got into bed. In moments, he was asleep.

• • •

At 5 bells, Terrier awoke Revin with a tub of hot water for bathing. Revin washed gratefully and then reclined in the bath. He wistfully remembered Momo bringing him a cup of coffee last time, but acknowledged to himself that it wasn't reasonable to expect the Queen to fetch and carry for him. But suddenly the adjoining door popped open and Momo breezed in carrying a cup of coffee.

"Are you decent?" she sang out, with a wink.

"I am not," Revin said, laughing.

She handed him the cup of coffee, which he gratefully accepted and sipped.

"The Summit begins at 10 bells," she said. "After breakfast, we should plan our strategy."

"Yes, Your Majesty," Revin said. "I'll be ready."

• • •

At 10 bells, Revin stood in the Portrait Gallery just behind Their Majesties and to the right of Queen Momoire. The delegates filed in and took seats. Revin went through the audience, trying to remind himself of names. He had met most of them at the reception the night before, but could only remember names for half.

"Welcome Delegates," the King began. "Today, we are here to discuss how to move forward after the disastrous failure of the attack by Harway on Havelock. As you have undoubtedly heard, Havelock triggered

Etheric Storm Generators that disrupted the invasion force, destroyed the capital of Harway, and killed my father — King Reginald.

"Through fortuitous chance, just before the assassination of the King, Momo and I wed to cement the alliance between our two island nations. But we find ourselves in a delicate situation with no clear plan nor leader. We come to you to solicit your input and seek consensus for a plan.

"We have asked our Chief of Staff, Sir Revin Minerson of Devishire, to lead this meeting."

Revin stood and cleared his throat.

"Welcome, honored delegates," he began. "As you know, we are facing a crisis. After the catastrophic defeat of the invasion force and the monstrous attack on Harway's capital that claimed the life of King Reginald, we need to identify a path forward."

Revin briefly introduced the Professor, who spoke for several minutes about the Etheric Storm Generator, which was still new to many. He ended with a brief warning.

"Although Harway captured the eternite mine that we believe was the source of their material for the generators," he said. "We don't know how many devices they constructed or how much eternite they recovered. Or, indeed, whether they discovered other sources on other islands — or on Havelock itself."

Revin thanked the Professor and seeing hands raised, opened the floor for comments and questions.

"Viscount Metterwin of Westland," Revin said, choosing someone whose name he remembered. "You have the floor."

"Thank you, Sir Revin," he said. "Why is there any question? We must crush Havelock. The Duke has demonstrated we have no choice but to take him down."

There was a murmur of assent from the entire body.

"But who will lead the assault?" said a man who didn't wait to be recognized. Suddenly there were raised voices and shouts, as various names were shouted out.

"Order!" Revin shouted over everyone. "I will have order!"

Voices subsided and Revin continued.

"Count Cindakor, you are recognized and have the floor."

"The only one who can lead the expeditionary force is the Baron. I believe he is the only one that can bring us together."

Murmurs of support came from the assembled body. Revin looked toward the Baron.

"Milord?" Revin said, inviting him to speak.

The Baron rose and turned to address the body.

"I am honored by your trust," he said. "But I don't believe we have a sufficient army — even when combined with forces that remain from Harway — to assure victory. And I will not commit us to a protracted invasion that we might not win."

Silence from the assembled delegates and a sense of gloom descended upon the room.

"What if I knew how to even the odds?" Revin said.

The Baron looked at him sharply. Revin stood up straight and held firm.

"Upon your word," the Baron said. "Then I will be your most humble servant."

The room erupted in cheers as Revin shook hands with the Baron.

•　　　•　　　•

The *Queen* approached the coast of Havelock in the pre-dawn hours at a high altitude and then turned to skirt the coast. Grip cranked down the ramp while Will helped Revin strap himself into the glider.

"Unassisted, you should have no problem reaching the coast," Will said. "But even a small towline will probably be enough to keep you aloft until the city."

"And you'll be ready?" Revin asked.

"As soon as the Baron launches the assault, we will watch for your signal."

With this assurance, Will gave Revin a pat on the shoulder and helped him out onto the ramp. Revin had worn two extra shirts for some extra insulation, but was still shivering, though not entirely from the cold. He was familiar with heights, having been on airships many times. But jumping off of them was something else altogether. He pulled out the monocle he had gotten from Will and fixed it over his eye. Then, taking a deep breath, he took a running start and leapt off the ramp into open air.

At first, he panicked when it felt like he was going straight down. He struggled to get his feet up into the supports, heart racing. But once he'd picked up a little speed, he felt the glider start to gain lift and the dive flattened out into a long glide.

With the monocle, he studied the etheric flows and made an attachment to a strong flow going the right direction. He felt the glider pick up speed and it actually started to climb! He grew increasingly confident as he overflew the coast.

He had chosen to approach the city from the East, to stay well clear of the aerodrome, but it meant approaching the city from an unfamiliar direction. He strained his eyes, trying to look for familiar landmarks and trying to spot Lidja's apartment building. He was practically straight above it when he finally recognized it. He panicked for a moment, feeling like he'd missed his chance. But then he just cut the towline and began turning lazy circles, dumping altitude, until he was just above the rooftops.

The mansard roof on the building with Lidja's apartment looked forbidding to land on, but the adjacent building had a large, long flat roof. Revin lined himself up, then realized, with the wind behind him, he was flying far too fast and would overshoot the building. In a panic, with the roof of Lidja's apartment rushing at him, he found another etheric stream and made the biggest towline he could. He squeezed his eyes shut as he started to climb and just barely cleared the roof.

After climbing for a few minutes, he cut the line and looped back for another try. Heading into the wind this time, he lined up well in advance of the roof and judged the height better. As he cleared Lidja's roof, he dropped his feet out of the supports and touched down at a run. He almost lost his balance and nearly tumbled, but just managed to stay on his feet and bring the glider to a stop. He had never wanted to kiss the ground more.

After unstrapping himself, he ran to the edge of the building and, looking down a few feet, identified the window of Lidja's bedroom. He pulled a few copper bits out of his pocket and threw one against her window. And then another and another, until he saw she was opening the window to look out and see what was going on. She looked up and caught sight of Revin and her face broke into a huge smile.

"Revin!" she squealed. "What are you doing here?"

"May I come in?"

"Yes, of course!"

Revin sprang across the narrow gap between the buildings and scrambled over to the window and climbed inside. Lidja seized him in a hug and pulled him down onto the bed.

"Oh! Oh! Oh!" she said, kissing his face over and over. "I've missed you so much! But, look at you! What happened to you?"

She put hands on both sides of his face and looked at his black eye and bruises that were finally starting to fade. She kissed his eyes very gently.

"I'm here," Revin said. "And that's all that matters. What's been happening here?"

"Oh, it's really bad, Revin," Lidja said. "There are soldiers everywhere now. They're stopping everyone and searching everything."

"Are you still driving the coach for the Seneschal?" Revin asked.

"No," Lidja said sadly. "They said that until the crisis is over I should stay home."

"It just means I'll have you all to myself," Revin said. Lidja hugged him even tighter and then kissed him on his mouth when he tried to say something else.

"But there is something I want to do," he said, when Lidja finally came up for air.

"Mmmmm," Lidja said, giving him little kisses on his neck and throat and working her way lower.

"And it's dangerous," he continued as she began to unbutton his shirts.

"Mm-hmm," she said, reaching around to unhook his chest binding.

"And I'll need your help," he said.

"Mm-hmm," she agreed as she kissed him on his chest and belly.

"I'm not sure you're taking this seriously," Revin said.

"Hmm," she said, loosening his trousers and working her way even lower.

Revin closed his eyes, leaned back, and gave himself over to her completely.

•   •   •

Later, while Lidja fixed them some sandwiches, Revin climbed back onto the other building, collapsed the glider as the Professor had shown him how to do, and, when Lidja was ready, he lowered it to her and they slipped it through the window to keep it safe and out of sight.

"Now," she said, while they munched the sandwiches. "You're going to need a disguise. They'll be watching for you."

"This sounds familiar," he said, rolling his eyes.

They looked through Lidja's closet. Lidja was only a little shorter than Revin and she had a couple of dresses that fit surprisingly well — if a little tight across the chest. He selected a light country dress decorated with little embroidered flowers. He let his hair down and Lidja found a barrette for him to keep the hair out of his eyes. After packing some food and supplies, they headed out.

The streets were nearly deserted but for soldiers patrolling. Or, rather, looking for trouble. They tried to hurry and be unobtrusive. Revin felt naked to be without his sword — let alone wearing a dress. He and Lidja ducked into a store when a party of soldiers approached on their side of the street. The owner hustled them behind the counter and encouraged them to hide when the soldiers peered through the windows. After the soldiers passed on, they thanked the owner profusely. Revin offered him money, but he refused.

Eventually, they reached the shop of Mr. Darkpony.

"Why, hello, Lidja," he said. "What can I do for you?"

"We need to rent a couple of horses," she said.

"I'm sorry, but there's an order that everything needs to be kept back in case our stock is requisitioned for the war. So I can't rent horses right now."

"But it's an emergency," Lidja pleaded. "My sister's boyfriend beats her and she needs to get away before he kills her."

She pointed at Revin's black eye and arms that were still fantastic shades of yellow and purple. Revin tried to look sad and terrified and even managed to produce a few tears.

"I'm so sorry," he said. "I really can't … They'd shut me down."

Lidja looked discouraged and Revin stared at the floor like he was devastated.

"Look," he said, finally. "I can't rent you horses from here. But I have two horses at my country house that you could borrow. They haven't been ridden much lately, so they might be a little difficult to work with, but you know what you're doing with horses."

"Oh, thank you!" Lidja said.

Revin looked up hopefully and smiled shyly. Mr. Darkpony beamed.

An hour later, Darkpony closed the shop and led Lidja and Revin through the streets. When they turned a corner, they were confronted at a guard checkpoint.

"What's your business?" asked a bored guard.

"I've hired these women to work at my country house," Darkpony said. "And I'm taking them to get them started."

"Your name?" the guard asked, picking up a clipboard.

"Hirus Darkpony."

"Lidja Relsing," Lidja said.

"Raveena Relsing," Revin said.

"R, R, R..." the guard mused, looking through the list. Then he looked at each of them carefully and flipped through a few pages at the end. Revin twitched when he saw one was a wanted poster with a fair drawing of his face. But the guard seemingly did not recognize him.

"OK," he said, waving them through.

Darkpony led them out of town and into a gentle landscape of rolling grassland past the outskirts. After a half hour, they reached a comfortable cottage that had several outbuildings and a barn with a paddock beyond.

"Welcome!" Darkpony said, leading them around back. "Let me take you to meet the horses."

He opened the gate and led them inside the paddock.

"The sorrel is a gelding named 'Honey' and he's sweet and gentle," he said. "The black one is a warmblood named 'Bastard' and, well, you'll see."

Lidja went up to the sorrel and had him eating out of her hand in moments.

"Sugar cube," she explained.

The other horse, a stallion, was another matter. He laid his ears back at Lidja as she approached. She stopped and watched his body language. For a couple of minutes, she just stood there and waited, eyes down and her posture unthreatening. Eventually, his ears lifted and he shuffled forward. She offered him a sugar cube, which he accepted and, then she rubbed his nose and began to whisper to him. The stallion snorted and then put his head over her shoulder and pulled her up against his chest. She patted his shoulder and back.

"I think we're going to get along just fine," Lidja said.

Revin started to walk over toward Lidja when the horse suddenly reached over her and snapped at him. He stumbled backward and Darkpony caught him and set him on his feet.

"You're okay, little Miss," he said. "Lidja can handle him and you'll be fine on the sorrel. Just keep an eye on that Bastard. Now, let's go inside and have some dinner and I'd be happy to have you stay here for the night."

Inside, they found that Darkpony's wife, Missy, had seen them arrive and had added two more place settings to the table for dinner. Revin kept quiet during dinner, letting Lidja and Hirus carry the conversation, talking about horses and horse breeding. He snuck a glance at Missy, who winked and then rolled her eyes at Hirus and Lidja oblivious to everything except horses. Revin smiled cautiously.

"Your boyfriend did that?" Missy asked in a lull in the conversation. "Men are terrible. They're all beasts."

"They're ... They're not all bad," Revin said.

"And this one is the worst," Missy said, shaking the shoulders of her husband. "Take them to the guest room, dear, while I clean up after dinner."

He led them to a tiny room that had one small bed.

"Since you're sisters, I hope this is OK."

"This is wonderful," Lidja said. "You've been more than generous."

As soon as the door was closed, Lidja grabbed Revin and pulled him onto the bed.

"Ooh! I can hardly stand it! You're so cute when you're a girl," she whispered into his ear. "You're so shy and demure. But let's see what happens when the lights go off."

"Rowr," Revin growled in her ear, slipping his hand under her shirt.

"Oh, it's true!" she groaned a little later. "Men are all beasts!"

"Ssh!" Revin whispered. "We're supposed to be sisters here!"

●　　　●　　　●

The next morning, they came out to find that Missy had fixed them a hot breakfast. Hirus was still in bed, so they had a nice quiet meal with Missy. Afterward, she took them out to find the tack for the horses.

"I thought I would want to ride Honey more," she sighed. "It was my idea to get the horses. But I don't ride him like I ought to. So I'm really glad you're going to take him out for a bit. I think he'll really like it."

"I promise I'll bring them home safe and sound," Lidja said. "Your trust means so much to me."

"And you watch that Bastard," Missy warned. "He's well named."

"Oh, he's just a big softy," Lidja said, patting his shoulder as the horse reached over and grabbed a hank

of Revin's hair and yanked it hard, throwing him onto the ground.

"Oh, yeah," Revin said, as he struggled back to his feet, rubbing his head. "This is going to be great."

After saddling the horses, Missy gave them a lunch to enjoy on the road. Hirus came out in time to wave at them as they set out on the road.

Revin had never ridden on horseback before (not counting the mine pony he'd ridden as a child). Lidja helped him quickly master the basics. He was struck by how much he'd missed when he'd traveled this route by coach before. Being on horseback was amazing — to be out in the world seeing, hearing, and experiencing everything. Revin excitedly pointed at something and then jerked his hand back when Bastard snapped at his fingers – and nearly got them. After that, he kept a wary eye for when the evil horse would try to sidle up closer.

When they stopped for lunch, Revin found he could barely walk. Being unaccustomed to being on horseback and wearing a dress, his thighs were red and chafed. Lidja nearly broke down in hysterics watching Revin try to walk with his legs apart. Luckily, she had thought to pack a little skin cream and, after liberal application, Revin took the opportunity to duck into the bushes to change out of the dress and put on his regular attire. Once again, he gave thanks to Cedric for making such excellent clothes that were not only stylish and functional, but actually fit.

By mid-afternoon, they reached the lonely tree where Revin and the Professor had been ambushed. Revin took a few minutes and acted out the whole drama for Lidja — who was appropriately shocked and horrified. Then they pressed on and, shortly after nightfall, reached the farm where Lidja had been indentured.

"Do you think we can sneak in to talk to the workers without the bosses becoming aware?" Revin asked.

"Oh, we can probably get to the bunkhouses," Lidja said. "The bosses lock up and then they get drunk, usually. I don't know how we'll get a key, though."

"What kind of pirate do you take me for?" Revin said, drawing himself up. "I was taught to pick locks by a master!"

Lidja covered her mouth with her hand and tried to stifle her laughter.

They left the horses staked out across the road and then slipped under cover of darkness to the first bunkhouse. It took Revin several tries — making him start to sweat — before he succeeded in picking the lock. When they opened the door, they found someone standing with a chunk of wood ready to wallop him on the head.

"Stop! Stop!" Lidja said, darting in ahead of Revin with her hands raised.

"Lidja! Lidja!" everyone started yelling. "Lidja! Lidja!"

Everyone surrounded her hugging and crying.

"They told us you were dead!" a man said. "We were so worried! We didn't know what happened to you!"

"I'm sorry I couldn't tell you anything," she said, crying freely. "But it was Revin who rescued me! And Revin has something he wants to tell you."

"Sorry," said the man with the chunk of wood. "Sometimes they come in at night when they're drunk to try to grab girls. Thank you so much for saving Lidja."

"Listen up, everyone!" Revin yelled over the noise. "If you want to do something about the unjust system of indenture on Havelock, there is a chance right now to fight."

"Fight?" said one man. "What can we do? They'll call out the army on us and kill us all."

"The army is going to be busy fighting Belleriand and Harway," Revin said. "If we attack while the army is occupied, we can take control and then we can be in a favorable position to negotiate."

"What good will that do?" an older woman asked. "The nobles are all the same."

"There's a new king," Revin said. "King Stewart. And Queen Momoire. They have agreed to meet with your representatives and to write a constitution that ensures fair treatment for everyone."

"This is bullshit," said another man. "You're just going to get us killed."

"Weren't you also the one who said you could trust the new boss?" Lidja asked. "Didn't you also say they weren't going to lock the doors anymore?"

Everyone laughed and the man slunk off into the shadows.

"I'm not saying it will be easy," Revin said. "Or without risk. But there's a chance here. If we act fast."

"What do we need to do?"

"We need to get as many people to the capital as fast as possible," Revin explained. "The armies from Harway and Belleriand are going to be landing soon led by the Baron."

Suddenly a murmur ran through the room.

"The Butcher Baron?" someone asked.

"Once that happens," Revin continued. "We want to hit the capital from behind and capture it before the army does. Then we'll be in the best position to negotiate favorable terms. Are you with me?"

"This is a lot to take in," a woman said. "Who are you and why should we believe you?"

"You should believe him first of all because he's my boyfriend," Lidja said. "He's the pirate who stole my heart.

"But he is also Sir Revin. He was the King's special envoy. And he's the chief of staff for Queen Momoire."

"I'm in!" said one.

"Me too!" said another.

"Us too! Us too" said more.

"Okay! Okay!" Revin said. "We need to make a plan. We need to liberate everyone on this farm first. And then divide up and hit every farm between here and the capital."

In little more than half an hour, they had broken the locks off the rest of the bunkhouses and assembled as a mob surrounding the guard house. Armed with hoes and mattocks — or in many cases, just sticks — they charged the building with Revin at the lead. The door fell and the guards were indeed mostly drunk or asleep and fell quickly to the mob. The most violent and hated bosses were dragged out and beaten to death. Others were captured and tied up. Revin felt sickened by the brutality of the aftermath, but given what he'd seen of their suffering, he felt little sympathy for the bosses that had maintained the cruel system.

Searching through the house for weapons, they found a cache of swords and spears that were quickly passed out among the most experienced of the men. Revin found a smallsword that fit his hand well enough and took it.

"Now, get the wagons out and start heading for the capital," Revin said. "And liberate every indentured worker on the way!"

An enthusiastic cheer went up from the workers, in high spirits after their easy victory. As the workers hitched up wagons and started organizing to move to the next set of farms, Revin and Lidja snuck back to the horses and struck out cross country toward where Revin understood the allied forces were landing.

They made good time by night in the grassland, but when they reached a more wooded area, they stopped and curled up together in the damp grass and slept fitfully until sunrise.

•   •   •

As Revin and Lidja approached the pickets of the Baron's invasion force, a looped rope snaked out and grabbed Lidja and dragged her off her horse. Four men sprang out of a concealed position that had been dug into the earth in the undergrowth. A man grabbed her and put an arm around her neck.

"Get down, mister," he said. "Nice and easy, or I'll break her neck. Easy now!"

Revin slipped off the back of Honey and kept his hands raised as the men approached. But they hadn't counted on Bastard. The man with his arm around Lidja's neck started screaming when Bastard bit his neck where it joined the shoulder. Hard. Then the horse reared up, trumpeting, and brained one of the other men with flying hooves. Then he landed hard, trampling the first man — Revin heard bones crunch as the man's screams were suddenly cut off. Lidja ended up on the ground with Bastard standing over her with his head down and ears pinned back. The other two men turned their backs to Revin in the face of this terrifying new enemy. Revin drew his sword and calmly ran one of them through the back. But before he could kill the last one, the man took to his heels and fled the field.

Lidja got to her feet and wrapped her arms around Bastard's neck and hugged him, whispering her quiet words of encouragement until he was calmer. Revin kept his distance until she held Bastard's reins in her hand. Then, leading Honey, Revin walked forward with Lidja until they reached the picket line and he identified them to the soldiers.

Passed by the sentries, Revin and Lidja arrived at the command tent. The Baron glanced up over his glasses as Revin entered. He finished a note and a courier carried it off. Then the Baron turned his full gaze on Revin who snapped to attention in spite of himself.

"Report!"

"We have successfully initiated a revolt of the indentured workers of Havelock," Revin said. "Whether this fizzles or becomes an avalanche remains to be seen. But we've told them to attack the capital in two day's time."

"We will attack tomorrow," the Baron said. "And hopefully that will draw their forces and attention toward us, giving the farm workers the opportunity to attack from behind."

"I think they'll need some expert leadership," Revin said.

"I disagree, Sir Revin," the Baron said. "If we had weeks to train them, they could take advantage of expertise. But as things stand, they're going to be a mob."

"Someone should still go to help them coordinate," Revin said. "I'll go by myself."

"Pardon me," Lidja said from the doorway.

Revin and the Baron looked over at her.

"And who are you, Miss?" the Baron asked, standing.

"I'm sorry," Revin said. "I should have introduced you. If you please, Milord Baron Curtis Belthingstone of Belleriand, allow me to introduce Miss Lidja Relsing of Havelock."

"How do you do, Miss?" the Baron replied.

"I'm pleased to make your acquaintance, Milord," Lidja said, curtsying.

"You were saying, Miss?"

"I want to take the horses back," she said. "We borrowed them from Mr. Darkpony, but his cottage is in the path of the advancing farm workers. He and Missy will be in danger."

"You're right, Lidja," Revin said. "We should go immediately."

"Can you indicate on this map where you're going?" the Baron asked.

Revin looked over the map with him and pointed out the area as best as he could remember.

"Good. Get a hot meal before you go," the Baron said. "And be careful."

After visiting the mess tent, they slipped back out through the lines the way they had come and started making the long trek around the city toward the Darkponys' cottage. They kept moving even after dark, at points leading the horses on foot over the rougher terrain to avoid the roads where they assumed there might be checkpoints and guards.

The sky was growing light when they arrived in the pre-dawn hours back at the Darkpony cottage. They took the horses out back. Lidja removed Honey's tack and showed Revin how to brush him. While he occupied himself doing that, she took care of Bastard. She made sure the horses were well supplied with fodder. Then Revin and Lidja went around to the front of the cottage and sat on the front porch in the early sun while the birds called from the treetops. Revin felt conflicted knowing that just a few miles away, the attack on the capital was probably commencing. Lidja leaned up against Revin and he leaned his head over onto hers.

"You two are just too cute," Missy said suddenly from the kitchen window.

"Missy!" Lidja said, jumping up. "Let me introduce my boyfriend Revin."

She looked at Revin for a moment, then smiled.

"Hi, Raveena — I mean, Revin!" she said with a wink. "You still have a black eye. Don't worry — I won't tell anyone. Won't you both join us for breakfast?"

Hirus wasn't up yet, but they joined Missy at the kitchen table for a light breakfast with coffee. In a few minutes, Hirus came out, blearily wiping the sleep out of his eyes. He perked up when he saw Lidja.

"Is your sister OK?" he asked. "Is this your brother?"

"This is my boyfriend, Revin" Lidja said, taking Revin's hand. Missy just smiled and sipped her coffee.

"We came back to warn you that the war is starting," Revin told them. "There is an army attacking the capital from Harway and Belleriand. But indentured farm workers have revolted and are moving toward the capital from this side."

"What should we do?"

"To be honest," Revin said, scratching his head. "I'm not quite sure what to do. I don't think it would be a good idea to go into the city since fighting has already started. And I don't think any other direction would necessarily be better. I'm hoping that when the farm workers get here, we can persuade them to bypass us. But I suggest you get ready and pack a bag in case we need to run."

Revin and Lidja kept watch while Hirus and Missy got packed. As they were finishing, Revin saw some farm workers appear on the road. Behind them were more and more and more. It was a veritable army advancing. They fanned out as they approached the cottage, evidently planning to search the outbuildings. Revin went out to meet them.

When he showed himself, some of the farm workers charged toward him with spears raised.

"Hold!" Revin called, raising his hands. "We're on your side. I'm here to lead you into the capital."

They continued to advance threateningly toward Revin.

"We're on your side!" Revin called again. Then Lidja joined him.

"Lidja!" someone farther back called. "That's Lidja!"

"Lidja! Lidja!" people called. The men advancing put up their spears.

"You should stay here, Lidja, to help keep Missy and Hirus safe in case more come this way," Revin said. "I'll go with this group and try to help coordinate."

•　　•　　•

Revin walked at the head of a long column of farm workers armed mostly with mattocks, shovels, and spears. As they advanced on the outskirts of the capital, most people went into their homes and locked the doors. But some, bringing their own weapons, came out and joined the workers advancing on the capital.

As they approached the checkpoint at the town limits, they saw only three guards. The guards took one look at the approaching mob and abandoned their post, fleeing toward the city center.

Revin and the mob reached the central plaza and found the Executive Building ringed with fortifications. At the top of the building, an airship awaited.

The mob was reluctant to charge into the fortified positions. A few crossbow bolts emphasized their trepidation and the farm workers confined themselves to yelling insults and shaking their tools outside of crossbow range. The soldiers, evidently an elite guard for the Duke, impassively held their positions with good discipline. Revin went along the line of farm workers, exhorting them to hold firm and wait until more workers arrived. As he reached the end of the line, he saw another body of workers arriving from the east road. He sprinted toward them and spoke with their leaders as they approached, telling them to wait for a signal to all charge together. Then he sprinted back as he saw yet another group arriving and he explained again.

As each group arrived, Revin tried to count as best he could and judged that there were four to five hundred farm workers. He couldn't see how many soldiers were concealed behind the fortifications, but he judged there couldn't be more than a hundred. Stepping out in front of the lines, Revin drew his sword, raised it over his head, as he'd told them he would, and then lowered it to point at the enemy and screamed, "Charge!" The line leapt forward as one.

Revin blended in with the others running toward the lines as a wave of crossbow bolts struck the line. Dozens fell, but the line swept forward and hit the lines of sandbags. Behind him, the soldiers had spears and drawn swords and the first dozen farm workers were cut down. Howls and screams filled the air. But then the numbers of the mob began to tell. Revin saw soldier after soldier struck down with the crude weapons of the farm workers. The soldiers fell back in an orderly process at first, but as the farm workers pressed them, the soldiers broke ranks and were routed into the building.

They tried to bar the entrance, but the farm workers' mattocks made short work of the doors and pried them off their hinges. With his naked sword in hand, Revin sprinted to the stairs and started climbing. He reached the top and came out onto the roof to see the Seneschal standing on the ramp of an airship with the name *Jolly Jenny* painted across the bow.

"Please, Your Highness," the Seneschal begged. "Let me come with you!"

Two soldiers inside the airship threw him off. The Seneschal tried picking himself up off the roof, then shrank back as he saw Revin advance.

The towlines shifted and the airship began to rise. Revin grabbed his signal mirror and scanned the sky until he spotted the *Queen* standing off-and-on near the Baron's army engaged south of the city. Revin began flashing the *Queen* until he saw her turn toward him. Then he turned his full attention to the Seneschal.

"Sir Revin," the Seneschal pleaded. "Don't kill me! I was just following orders. I always tried to help you, don't you remember?"

Farm workers arrived at the top of the building. Revin had to prevent them from killing the Seneschal until the *Queen* touched down. Revin gestured toward the ramp with his sword and the man gratefully fled on board the ship until he saw Will.

"Professor Dirge!" the Seneschal whimpered. "But you're dead!"

"Keep him under guard," Revin said, following him on board. "And follow that airship! The Duke is getting away!"

"You heard him!" Will called, running to the remmer deck.

The *Queen* had barely risen when Will began personally making the biggest, fattest towlines Revin had ever seen. Men on the roof flattened themselves or were bowled over as the Queen leapt forward still only two or three feet above the building.

Revin ran to the observation deck and looked ahead to the Duke's airship, practically just a point on the horizon.

"Two points to starboard!" he called to Grip who was manning the cockpit.

"Two points to starboard!" Grip relayed to the remmer deck.

Revin felt the floor shift under his feet as the *Queen* turned slightly to the right.

For three hours, the *Queen* made steady progress closing the distance. Sensing the inevitable, the Duke's ship ducked into clouds.

"Hold!" Revin called from the observation deck.

"Hold!" Grip called to the remmer deck.

Towlines winked out and the *Queen* drifted with the wind while Revin kept watch. Five minutes. Ten minutes. Fifteen minutes.

Revin got antsy and was just about to call for them to push forward when he saw the airship emerge from the clouds, far below making a run for the south.

"Forty five degrees to port! Full speed! Descend!" Revin yelled loud enough that, even before Grip could speak, huge towlines appeared and the *Queen* sprang ahead above the clouds and stooped on the *Jenny* like a falcon.

"Clear the decks!" Grip cried. "Ready for action! Boarding parties prepare!"

The *Queen* closed on its quarry. A fat towline sparked out and grabbed their quarry and stopped it dead in its tracks. The *Queen* came alongside in moments and grapnels tied them together. The boarding parties attacked fore and aft, cutting through the sides of the airship and charging aboard.

Revin followed the pirates with his sword drawn while boarding an airship for the first time in his life. He nearly slipped on his first step where a pirate had fallen, run through the neck, his blood sprayed liberally across the walls and floor. He heard the ring of swordplay farther down the corridor. Revin opened doors into cabins as he ran along the corridor. Empty. Empty. Empty. He worked his way back through the airship. He pulled open the last door in First Class and found a man huddled among trunks and boxes.

Soft and pale with blonde hair, his plump fingers bore multiple rings. He crouched among bags and chests loaded with treasure.

"Don't kill me! Don't kill me!" he pleaded when Revin placed himself *en garde*.

"Grip!" Revin bellowed. "To me!"

In moments, Grip was at hand.

"Confine this criminal," Revin said. "He must stand trial."

"Yessir," Grip said. "I will assure that he lives to stand trial."

Grip dragged the Duke away.

Left alone in the room, Revin looked around at bags and boxes and chests filled with treasure. Treasure looted from Havelock. Revin was filled with righteous indignation, remembering the indentured workers laboring under the lash to accumulate this monster's wealth. But then he spotted something and, after a moment's battle with his conscience, he shrugged and pocketed it. Stepping back in the corridor, he felt a weight lift off him he hadn't realized was there until its absence left him feeling elated and liberated.

The sounds of combat faded as the last of the soldiers fell.

"The ship is ours, Your Excellency" Will reported, coming from amidships.

"Stuff it with your titles," Revin laughed.

Will looked in the room and whistled.

"What are your plans for the treasure?" he asked.

"I'm going to pretend I didn't see it and leave it entirely in your hands," Revin said.

"But ... But I'm a pirate!" Will said, astonished.

"You know what will happen to it if it goes back to Belleriand," Revin said. "You're a pirate. But I know where your heart truly lies."

They grinned at one another and shook hands.

It took another hour to treat the wounded pirates, and get the *Jolly Jenny* ready to travel back to Havelock.

The *Queen* and *Jenny* arrived back at the Executive Building around midnight. The fighting seemed to be over. Everything was quiet. Revin went down the stairs through the empty, abandoned building and emerged into the plaza, where he found an odd tableau. People jammed the plaza. On one side, backed by ranks of well-disciplined soldiers, stood the Baron. Encircled by hundreds of unruly, ebullient farm workers, Lidja and Darkpony were speaking with him.

"What you're requesting is … extraordinary," the Baron said.

"It is not!" Lidja said, standing toe-to-toe with the Baron and fixing him with a fierce stare. "It's fundamental to what we require. There must be an equal voice for common people."

Revin walked up and put his arm around Lidja, who shrieked with relief and hugged Revin for all she was worth.

A huge cheer went up among the farm workers.

"Revin! Revin! Revin!" they chanted.

"What she said," Revin said. "We have two demands. The system of indenture must be ended. And there must co-equal representation for common people in government."

"You know Her Majesty's mind," the Baron said. "If you are able to speak for her, we can resolve this now."

"We are victorious!" Revin shouted.

And everyone cheered.

Revin reached into his pocket and brought out the ring he had taken from the Duke's hoard. He knelt down on one knee, before an astonished Lidja, and proffered it to her.

"Lidja Relsing, I love you. Will you marry me?"

A collective gasp went up from the assembled crowd and then there was silence. The Baron grinned.

"Oh, Revin!" she squealed, hugging him. "Yes! Yes! Yes!"

Revin was engulfed by a huge roar of approval from the crowd.

•   •   •

Two days later, the *Queen of Belleriand* landed at the aerodrome on Belleriand. Will gave Revin a big hug as he readied himself to assume his duties as Chief of Staff for the Queen of Belleriand. Grip snatched Revin up and twirled him around in the air like he had for Momoire. Blushing, Revin hugged him tenderly and then tried not to cry as he descended the gangplank to step onto the soil of Belleriand. He emerged to find a gauntlet of guards in Belthingstone colors awaiting him that snapped to attention and escorted him to a coach for the short drive to Ravensbelth.

Youngman welcomed him graciously to the Belthingstone palace. Revin requested an audience with the Queen at her earliest convenience, then allowed Terrier to lead him to his chamber to freshen up and change clothes to meet with the Queen. He was still naked when she walked through the adjoining door into his room.

"Your Majesty!" Revin said, scandalized.

"Oh, Revin," she said, advancing on him and giving him a hug. "I'm so glad you're back!"

"I'm glad to be back too, Your Majesty," he said, trying to pull on some clothes.

"The prisoners arrived yesterday: The Duke of Havelock and his Seneschal."

"Good!"

"They seemed to think they had absconded with the bulk of the treasury of Havelock, yet when they arrived, there was no money."

"Huh," Revin said blushing, in spite of himself. "I guess they must have been mistaken."

"Mistaken," Queen Momoire growled. "Is that what you call that?"

"What else could have happened?" Revin asked, innocently.

"Hmm," the Queen temporized. "And I hear that, in my name, you signed off on creating some kind of government on Havelock that includes commoners? Is that true?"

"You were very enthusiastic about the idea, Your Majesty," Revin assured her.

"I can see that I'm going to need to keep you on a shorter leash," she said, scowling.

"But I did want to ask ..." Revin began.

"About your horse girl?" the Queen asked with a sharp glance. "Yes, of course. By all means, you can bring her along."

"Oh, she also needs to bring her horse. A wedding present from the new Prime Minister."

"I've heard rumors about this horse already. Is it really as vicious as everyone says?"

Revin blanched, remembering both his close personal calls with the diabolical horse and seeing it trample a man to death. He grimaced.

"The rumors truly don't do it justice, Your Majesty."

"And are William and Griphon really going to stay on Havelock?"

"Yes, Your Majesty," Revin said. "And the Professor. Now that there's a government of the people, they're going to go straight and help get the new government launched."

"They're really going to give up piracy?"

"Well, they aren't 'going straight' in the other way."

"Tell me about the man who's going to be the interim Prime Minister."

"That's Hirus Darkpony. He's a good choice. He's a successful businessman and has the respect of both nobles and commoners on Havelock. He'll be a good caretaker until they can get a functional government up and running."

"Once people here get wind of this idea, they're going to demand the same."

She gave him a long, hard look. Revin just grinned.

"Yes, Your Majesty."

"Well, as long as you're here to deal with it, I guess it will be alright."

"By your grace, Your Majesty," Revin said, bowing.

ABOUT THE AUTHOR

Steven D. Brewer has been a fan of science fiction and fantasy stories for as long as he can remember. He still remembers getting scolded for not reading chapter books in fourth grade because he was avidly consuming *The Hobbit* late at night, by flashlight under his covers. And he probably got his copy from his older brother and most important mentor.

Steven currently teaches scientific writing at the University of Massachusetts Amherst. He lives in Amherst, Massachusetts with his extended family.

ALSO IN THIS SERIES

THE THIRD TIME'S THE CHARM

BOOK ONE OF *REVIN'S HEART*

When an airship is hijacked by pirates, a young man with a secret loses his mentor ... and his future.

FOR THE FAVOR OF A LADY

BOOK TWO OF *REVIN'S HEART*

Even a pirate will stop at nothing to help his little sister.

STORM CLOUDS GATHER

BOOK THREE OF *REVIN'S HEART*

After the Queen of Belleriand encounters an etheric anomaly that threatens the airship, Revin is abducted. But by whom? And why?

CROSSING THE STREAMS

BOOK FOUR OF *REVIN'S HEART*

Revin and the Professor must go undercover to investigate a mysterious device that has the power to generate storms and may threaten their very existence.

THE END OF HIS ROPE

Book Five of *Revin's Heart*

Revin and the pirate crew travel to the heart of the kingdom to carry a dire warning about the dangers posed by the device that could end air travel forever.

THEN THEY FIGHT YOU

Book Six of *Revin's Heart*

When even the King's mandate isn't enough to bring the warring parties to the table, how far will Revin go to pursue peace?

Available in digital and trade paperback editions from
Water Dragon Publishing
waterdragonpublishing.com

YOU MIGHT ALSO ENJOY

THE ALCHEMIST DAUGHTER
by Paul S. Moore

When a concoction of ethers channels a little of their magic properties to one location, inspiration springs to life.

GREY MOTHER MOUNTAIN
by Elyse Russell

When her village is destroyed, an elderly woman seeks help from the last remaining dragon to get revenge.

SONGS OF A DEAD FOREST
by Travis Wade Beaty

Old songs can bring new life.

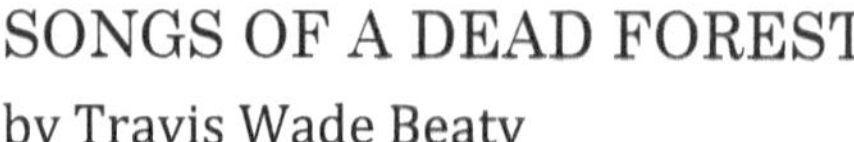

WAY CROSSER
by Mia Ram

After being thrown off-course by a savage storm, a crew of sailors find themselves enthralled by the mystery of a supernatural island and its graveyard of ships.

Available in trade paperback, digital, and audio editions from
Water Dragon Publishing
waterdragonpublishing.com